BARRON'S BOOK NOTES

JOHN STEINBECK'S
The Pearl

BARRON'S BOOK NOTES

JOHN STEINBECK'S

The Pearl

BY

Carol Forman

SERIES COORDINATOR

Murray Bromberg
Principal, Wang High School of Queens
Holliswood, New York

Past President
High School Principals Association of New York City

BARRON'S EDUCATIONAL SERIES, INC.

ACKNOWLEDGMENTS

Our thanks to Milton Katz and Julius Liebb for their contribution to the *Book Notes* series.

© Copyright 1985 by Barron's Educational Series, Inc.

All inquiries should be addressed to:
Barron's Educational Series, Inc.
250 Wireless Boulevard
Hauppauge, New York 11788

Library of Congress Catalog Card No. 85-3945

International Standard Book No. 0-8120-3534-8

Library of Congress Cataloging in Publication Data
Forman, Carol.
   John Steinbeck's The pearl.

   (Barron's book notes)
   Bibliography: p. 66
   Summary: A guide to reading "The Pearl" with a
critical and appreciative mind encouraging analysis
of plot, style, form, and structure. Also includes
background on the author's life and times, sample tests,
term paper suggestions, and a reading list.
   1. Steinbeck, John 1902–1968. Pearl.   [1. Steinbeck,
John, 1902–1968. Pearl.   2. American literature—History
and criticism]   I. Title.   II. Series.
PS3537.T3234P494   1985   813'.52   85-3945
ISBN 0-8120-3534-8

PRINTED IN THE UNITED STATES OF AMERICA

123   550   9876543

CONTENTS

CONTENTS

ADVISORY BOARD

We wish to thank the following educators who helped us focus our *Book Notes* series to meet student needs and critiqued our manuscripts to provide quality materials.

HOW TO USE THIS BOOK

You have to know how to approach literature in order to get the most out of it. This *Barron's Book Notes* volume follows a plan based on methods used by some of the best students to read a work of literature.

Begin with the guide's section on the author's life and times. As you read, try to form a clear picture of the author's personality, circumstances, and motives for writing the work. This background usually will make it easier for you to hear the author's tone of voice, and follow where the author is heading.

Then go over the rest of the introductory material—such sections as those on the plot, characters, setting, themes, and style of the work. Underline, or write down in your notebook, particular things to watch for, such as contrasts between characters and repeated literary devices. At this point, you may want to develop a system of symbols to use in marking your text as you read. (Of course, you should only mark up a book you own, not one that belongs to another person or a school.) Perhaps you will want to use a different letter for each character's name, a different number for each major theme of the book, a different color for each important symbol or literary device. Be prepared to mark up the pages of your book as you read. Put your marks in the margins so you can find them again easily.

Now comes the moment you've been waiting for—the time to start reading the work of literature. You may want to put aside your *Barron's Book Notes* volume until you've read the work all the way through. Or you may want to alternate, reading the *Book Notes* analysis of each section as soon as you have finished reading the corresponding part of the original. Before you move on, reread crucial passages you don't fully understand. (Don't take this guide's analysis for granted—make up your own mind as to what the work means.)

Once you've finished the whole work of literature, you may want to review it right away, so you can firm up your ideas about what it means. You may want to leaf through the book concentrating on passages you marked in reference to one character or one theme. This is also a good time to reread the *Book Notes* introductory material, which pulls together insights on specific topics.

When it comes time to prepare for a test or to write a paper, you'll already have formed ideas about the work. You'll be able to go back through it, refreshing your memory as to the author's exact words and perspective, so that you can support your opinions with evidence drawn straight from the work. Patterns will emerge, and ideas will fall into place; your essay question or term paper will almost write itself. Give yourself a dry run with one of the sample tests in the guide. These tests present both multiple-choice and essay questions. An accompanying section gives answers to the multiple-choice questions as well as suggestions for writing the essays. If you have to select a term paper topic, you may choose one from the list of suggestions in this book. This guide also provides you with a reading list, to help you when you start research for a term paper, and a selection of provocative comments by critics, to spark your thinking before you write.

THE AUTHOR AND HIS TIMES

Have you ever wondered where an author gets his ideas or inspiration?

In 1940, John Steinbeck and a good friend, Ed Ricketts, set out on a sailing trip that would later be described in Steinbeck's non-fiction work *The Sea of Cortez*. During the trip, Steinbeck heard a legend about the misfortunes of a poor fisherboy who had found a great pearl. Inspired by the legend, Steinbeck published *The Pearl* in a magazine in 1945 under the title "The Pearl of the World." The story was so successful that in 1947 it was published as a book and adapted as a film.

In his story, Steinbeck changed the young fisherboy of the legend into a man with a family. But the main idea remained the same—that a beautiful, valuable pearl brings only trouble and sadness, not peace or happiness, to a fisherman and his loved ones.

Steinbeck was an acute observer of human nature. He wrote about people he knew and about towns he had lived in. Prior to writing about these people, he would often live with them for a while and get to know their way of life. Most of his characters are down and out, isolated and oppressed. They give voice to the "struggle" theme of his novels—namely, the struggle between the poor and the wealthy, the weak and the strong, and between different types of civilization (for instance, European and Mexican).

His family was not rich, and Steinbeck would never forget his origins, even after he had become a celebrated writer. His father, a miller, had arrived in California shortly after the U.S. Civil War, and his mother was the daughter of immigrants from Ulster, Ireland. When Steinbeck was born on February 27, 1902, his parents settled in Salinas, a town in a fertile valley in western California, about 100 miles south of San Francisco.

Steinbeck's mother, a teacher in the Salinas school system, encouraged him to read at a very early age. Literature became his passion, and before he entered high school he was reading Jack London, the Bible, Gustave Flaubert's *Madame Bovary*, and Thomas Hardy's *The Return of the Native*. To earn money during the summer, Steinbeck worked as a hired hand on local ranches. This brought him into contact with Mexican-Americans and migrant workers, who earned little but worked long hours under the hot California sun. He discovered the harsh reality that one could survive these conditions only as long as one's strength held out. He also learned that workers were often treated poorly and without respect, and that they had little means of defending themselves.

As student, Steinbeck wrote for the school newspaper and enjoyed sports. In 1920, he entered Stanford University as an English major, wanting to be a writer but not quite sure how to become one. One thing was certain: the fun of fraternity parties held no attraction for the brawny, work-hardened Steinbeck, whose jobs had shown him a seamier side of life. Before long he was publishing poetry and short stories in the Stanford literary magazine.

After five years at Stanford, Steinbeck had completed fewer than half the credits necessary to graduate. He had taken on jobs in order to pay his tuition, and his curiosity about the outside world had helped keep him from fulfilling the university's graduation requirements. He had, however, taken a number of science courses and had met a teacher, Edith Mirrieles, who recognized his talent and encouraged him to write.

In 1925, he left California for a literary career in New York, but disliked the city. The financial situation that had plagued him in California was still a problem. Instead of pursuing a writing career, he found himself working as a cement mixer, capitalizing on the muscles he'd developed on ranches. After this job, he became a journalist with the New York *American*, a daily newspaper. These were the Roaring Twenties, and while some literary people were taking off on luxury cruises, Steinbeck was writing about the city's tenement dwellers, including newly arrived immigrants. He despised the cutthroat world of New York journalism at the time and hated running all over the city to cover what he considered unimportant events. He stuck it out for a while, though, because it gave him time to do creative writing. However, all of his stories were rejected. In 1927, having had enough of the city, he worked his way back to California as a deckhand on a freighter headed through the Panama Canal.

For the next two years, Steinbeck secluded himself in the mountains of California, writing and supporting himself with odd jobs. Finally, in 1929, his first novel, *Cup of Gold*, was published; it was an adventure novel about the life of the seventeenth-century English pirate, Sir Henry Morgan. Two months later, however, the stock market crashed and the country soon fell into the devastating Great Depression. For his two years' work, Steinbeck received a mere $250 advance from the publisher, and only about 1,500 copies were sold.

After marrying Carol Henning in 1930, Steinbeck met Ed Ricketts, a marine biologist, who owned the Western Biological Laboratory on Cannery Row in Monterey, California. Cannery Row was the location of fish canneries, and was also a hangout for "no goods" and "blots on the town" whom Steinbeck would later call Mack and the boys in his novel *Cannery Row* (1945). Steinbeck admired Ricketts because he was a "fountain of philosophy and science and art," held unconventional beliefs, and enjoyed an openness with the vagabonds of Cannery Row, who nicknamed him "Doc." Since Steinbeck wanted his novels to reflect an accurate portrait of life, he learned as much as he could about science from his new friend. In the process, he pushed on with his writing and developed what he called a spoken rather than a written style (see the Style section). Since he was most at ease writing about familiar people and places, he set his next two novels, *The Pastures of Heaven* (1932) and *To a God Unknown* (1933), in California's Salinas Valley, his childhood home.

From this point to the early 1950s, Steinbeck wrote and published consistently. His first major success came in 1933 when the monthly magazine *North American Review* published "The Red Pony" and three other short stories. After the success of the novel *Tortilla Flat* in 1935, Steinbeck's financial worries were over, and his fame as a writer was clinched in 1937 when *Of Mice and Men* appeared. The critics hailed him as one of America's leading writers, placing him among the "proletarian writers" who wrote about social problems of poor workers (proletarians). When you read *The Pearl*, set against the oppressive conditions under which Mexican Indians lived, you'll see why critics classified Steinbeck this way.

Troubled by what he saw from a distance, Steinbeck joined a group of Oklahomans migrating from drought and the effects of the Great Depression to what they hoped would be a better life in California. The harrowing experience led to *The Grapes of Wrath* (1939), a powerful novel for which Steinbeck won a Pulitzer Prize in 1940.

After the publication of *The Grapes of Wrath*, Steinbeck sailed with Ed Ricketts on an expedition to study the marine life in the Gulf of California, hoping to find universal patterns in marine species that would help him understand life in general. During this trip, Steinbeck heard the legend of the fisherboy who had found a pearl. He documented this trip in *The Sea of Cortez* (1941) and developed the fisherboy legend in *The Pearl*. When you read *The Pearl*, watch for details about the plant and animal life of the Gulf. Notice also the scientific metaphors (comparisons) and themes, which Steinbeck may have developed in part through discussions with Ed Ricketts.

Some critics felt that Steinbeck's later works— those following *The Pearl*—lacked the energy and conviction of his earlier books. Yet he won the prestigious Nobel Prize for Literature in 1962 and used his acceptance speech to strike back at critics who had attacked him. He argued that they were elitist, self-serving, and pessimistic. Pessimism was an outlook Steinbeck could not abide. He was an optimist who believed deeply in the perfectibility of man.

Steinbeck did not publish a novel again after winning the Nobel Prize, and died in New York on December 20, 1968. In his writing, he had deeply affected the conscience of Americans by forcing them to look at their most vulnerable and oppressed citizens. He made readers feel troubled, but he also made them remember their dreams and their belief in humanity.

THE NOVEL

The Plot

Kino, a poor Indian fisherman, lives on the Gulf of California with his wife Juana and infant son Coyotito. Their simple hut is made of brush, and the couple sleeps on mats thrown on the dirt floor, while Coyotito sleeps in a hanging box. Like others in their poor village, they depend on nature for survival. Despite the poverty, Kino is happy, honest, and hardworking.

As *The Pearl* begins, dawn is breaking. Kino watches the sun rise and listens to the sounds of the morning. In his mind, Kino hears the Song of the Family—an internal message that tells him all is well.

But within moments, a dangerous situation develops. A poisonous scorpion stings Coyotito, and the baby's screams draw people from all over the village. Juana insists that the doctor be called, but Kino knows the physician is of Spanish descent and considers himself above treating poor Indians. This does not satisfy Juana, who announces that if the doctor will not visit the village, then they will go directly to the doctor's house. Her independent spirit amazes the villagers, who join in a procession that accompanies Kino and Juana to the wealthy doctor's home. But the doctor refuses to treat Coyotito because Kino is too poor. Kino is so angry that he smashes his fist against the doctor's gate.

Later that day, while Kino and Juana are fishing

in the Gulf, Kino finds an enormous pearl—the Pearl of the World—and cries out in joy. He believes the pearl will make him rich and enable him to provide security for his family. But Kino discovers otherwise. The pearl stirs envy in the villagers, and that night Kino is attacked in his hut by a thief. The following day, he tries to sell the pearl to buyers in town, but he is offered only a small sum of money for it. The buyers all work for the same man. They know the pearl is worth a fortune but hope to buy it cheaply by pretending that it is worth little.

In his anger, Kino says he will sell his pearl in the capital city, where he believes he'll get a fair price. This amazes the villagers because Kino has never traveled so far. After dark that evening, Kino is attacked again. Juana is sure the pearl is evil and will destroy the family. During the night, she quietly removes it from the spot where Kino has hidden it and tries to throw it back into the ocean. He stops her before she succeeds and beats her for trying. As he returns to the hut, Kino is attacked again, this time by two men. He kills one of them, and the other escapes.

Because of the killing, Kino knows that he will be hunted as a murderer. As a result, he and Juana must leave the village immediately. Before they can escape, however, their canoe is destroyed and their hut is burned. They hide until the next night in the hut of Kino's brother, Juan Tomás. The following evening, Kino and Juana begin their flight to the capital. Soon they realize they are being pursued by three people, so they flee up the mountain and hide in a small cave. Their pursuers pitch camp in a clearing just below the cave. Kino decides the only way to survive is for him to kill the person on guard, take his rifle, and kill the other two, who are sleeping.

Kino goes to the pursuers' camp and is about to attack them when his infant son Coyotito cries out. Kino knows that he must spring immediately at his enemies, but he is a moment too late and one of them shoots toward the cave. There is a struggle and Kino kills all three of his enemies. The earlier shot has, however, killed Coyotito. The following afternoon the villagers witness the return of Kino and Juana, carrying the rifle and their dead child. Without a word to anyone, they walk through the village to the shore. Kino lays down the rifle, takes out the pearl, and throws it into the water.

The Characters

It is difficult to get to know the characters in *The Pearl* in the same way you might get to know the characters in other novels. They say very little, and you see them in relatively few situations. Their motivations seem to be based more on ancient habits or traditional social roles than on free choice. The characters are more like symbols for ideas than real people.

Steinbeck has often been criticized for failing to create more complex, realistic characters. On the other hand, some readers feel that Steinbeck's purpose—social criticism—is best served by characterizations that clearly represent a social group or an idea.

Kino
Kino is an honest, dignified pearl diver who works hard to support his family. He is a simple and

natural being who functions well in the traditional ways of the village. Kino is conscious of his poverty and knows that money could buy things he lacks. He hopes to find a pearl that will guarantee him future peace. Like most human beings, he wants to get ahead.

Kino depends on nature for his income. When the waters are rough, he cannot go diving. When the sun sets, his workday ends. The discovery of a great pearl changes Kino's life. The man who usually hears the Song of the Family—the harmonious, soothing message that all is well in life—begins to hear the voice of suspicion, the sounds of danger—the Song of Evil. This song is really a powerful internal voice that he hears when danger arises, which links him to his ancestors as a sort of built-in protection against death. It is Steinbeck's poetic way of referring to Kino's survival instinct.

On the other hand, Kino's intelligence and growth in social awareness help him realize that he and other Indians have been exploited by the rich and powerful. At first, instinctively, he senses the danger with the doctor and pearl buyers, but it is only after his brutal encounter with the trackers that he becomes aware of the extent of this exploitation. He comes to realize that human beings will kill in order to gain money and power.

As Kino moves away from his natural habitat, he becomes isolated. With the pearl in hand, he marches toward the city—a symbolic move toward a more complex civilization—in his belief that he can deal with "civilized" people. He lays claim to the benefits of civilization—power, money, an education for Coyotito—but soon realizes, when pursued by the trackers, that he is a victim of the very society in which he hopes to earn a profit. Some readers believe that Kino brings about his own downfall by going against the forces of nature. What do you think Kino should (or could) have done with the pearl? What do you think the end results would have been?

Kino loses more than his social innocence in the novel. He learns that he, too, can kill to protect his chance for wealth and power.

If the characters in *The Pearl* are symbols, what does Kino symbolize? Some readers say that Kino is the exploited but innocent man who loses his innocence when he tries to venture beyond his social boundaries. Others see Kino as the symbol of an honest, hard-working man destroyed by greed. Still others see him as a man unable to escape his fate.

Juana

Juana's relationship to Kino, her husband, is made clear in the first chapter of *The Pearl*. She is a loving and devoted wife, the stabilizing force in Kino's life. At first you may see her simply as subservient. But Juana has great inner strength and determination. For example, when Coyotito is bitten by the scorpion, Juana acts immediately and sucks out the poison. She also insists that they see the doctor—an unheard of event in the village.

Juana has a strong survival instinct where her family is concerned. When the doctor refuses to treat the baby, Kino responds by ineffectually punching the gate; Juana puts a seaweed poultice on the baby's shoulder. She responds with the same kind of direct action when she decides that the pearl is a threat to her family. She tries to throw it back in the sea.

If you are trying to decide what each character represents, you could say that Juana represents the integrity of a simple way of life. Throughout *The Pearl*, Juana appears to be in tune with nature and aware of what will save her family. Unlike Kino, who dreams of a new life, Juana does not believe in pursuing the unattainable.

Coyotito
Coyotito, the infant son of Kino and Juana, is a character whose purpose is to show nature in its most undeveloped form. In the struggle between nature and civilization—and between good and evil—Coyotito becomes the innocent victim of powers greater than himself.

The Doctor
The village doctor seems to be the perfect villain. He is someone to blame and hate, especially when he refuses to treat Coyotito and later even makes him ill. In the doctor's system of priorities, money counts more than human life or professional pride. The doctor also represents the biased behavior of persons of Spanish descent toward the Indians of Mexico. And, on a more general level, he symbolizes the arrogance of the powerful in all societies toward the powerless.

Despite this portrait of evil, however, Steinbeck adds another dimension when he describes the doctor's memories of life in Paris. He remembers the "hard-faced" woman he lived with as being "beautiful and kind," even though she was neither. Some see this passage as evoking sympathy

for the doctor by showing him as a pathetic figure.
Do you agree?

Juan Tomás

Juan Tomás is Kino's older and wiser brother. The
brothers share a simple, unaffected love that sus-
tains Kino in some of his most difficult times. Juan
Tomás is a storehouse of knowledge about the ways
of the world and methods of survival, and seems
to be a symbol of the collective wisdom of the Indian past. He gathers items for Kino's journey to
the capital, including the knife Kino uses to kill
the first tracker. He also covers for Kino in order
to confuse anyone who might be tempted to pur-
sue his brother.

The Priest

The priest is an undeveloped character. Like the
doctor, he appears only briefly in order to make a
claim to part of the pearl. He is not a source of
comfort or religious strength. The priest patronizes
the Indians, yet he will take their money. He seems
to stand for the general role of the Catholic Church
(as a partner of the Spanish Crown) in the con-
quest of Mexico and the subjugation of the Indians.

The Trackers

The trackers, or pursuers, symbolize human greed
at its worst. They want Kino's pearl and will kill
in order to get it. Steinbeck uses them to show
both the greed in humans and the irony of a social
system that oppresses the Indians further by making them hunt each other. (Two of the trackers are
Indians like Kino.)

Other Elements
SETTING

The events of *The Pearl* take place on an estuary (the mouth of a river) somewhere on the coast of Mexico, in the fictitious town of La Paz. If you look at a map, you'll see a long peninsula descending from the U.S. state of California. The peninsula, called Baja California, is part of Mexico and is separated from the rest of Mexico by the Gulf of California. (Another name for the Gulf of California is the Sea of Cortez, or Cortés.) Steinbeck traveled in this area with his friend Ed Ricketts in 1940 and described his experiences in *The Sea of Cortez* (1941).

Geographical features mentioned in *The Pearl* give clues to the setting. In a relatively short time, Kino walks from the estuary through desert scrub to mountains. This would be possible in Baja California.

Steinbeck doesn't tell you exactly when the events of the novel take place because they came from a legend. Although no date is given, you are told that the witnesses of Kino's return were the grandfathers of the present villagers. If Steinbeck heard the legend in 1940, that would set the story somewhere around 1900.

In order to understand Steinbeck's story, it will help you to know that Indians of Mexico had been under the domination of people of Spanish descent for some three hundred years at the time of the legend. A civil-religious hierarchy governed; although church (Roman Catholic) and state were outwardly separated, they worked together in many aspects of Mexican life. You'll see in the story how the priest and the pearl buyers act as allies in the social hierarchy, with the Indians at the bottom of the ladder. In many cases the Indians could not attend school or own land.

Although Spanish culture was imposed on Indians, the ancient religions and other aspects of the culture of the various tribes survived. Watch for places where you can see that Kino and Juana have merged both traditions—for example, Juana's combination of Catholic Hail Marys and ancient prayers.

One aspect of Mexican culture that plays a part in the novel is that of *mi tierra* (my land). The birthplace of an Indian had enormous significance. Many Mexicans, especially Mexican Indians, believed they were meant to stay where they were born, and they developed a special attachment to their birthplace. Knowing this concept might help you understand what a huge step Kino takes when he decides to leave La Paz for the capital.

THEMES

The following are themes of *The Pearl*.

1. THE STRUGGLE FOR EXISTENCE

One of the most important themes in *The Pearl* is that of Kino and Juana's struggle for survival. Even though their way of life may differ from yours, it contains the same kinds of struggles that everyone faces at some time—the struggle for food and shelter, and the struggle to fight off attacks from nature (the scorpion) and from other human beings, who burn their hut, destroy their canoe, hunt them down, and kill their child.

2. FREE WILL VS. DETERMINISM

Some people believe that human beings are never really free, because the course of their lives is determined by outside forces. Others insist that each person's life is formed by a series of choices.

Some aspects of Kino's life are, of course, determined for him. His race and social status are two examples. But other elements are the direct result of his actions—his determination to keep the pearl, his decision to go to the capital, and so on. Are Kino's decisions made freely, of his own accord, or are they based on factors beyond his control?

What does the end of Kino's story say about his ability to control his destiny? Is the finding of the pearl a quirk of fate? Without it, would Kino have any choices to make? All these questions may help you think about the role of choice in your own life, as well as Kino's.

3. SOCIAL CLASS

The Pearl raises the question of whether people should try to move or can move successfully from one social class to another. Specifically, should a poor Mexican Indian like Kino try to improve his status and live like the more prosperous city dwellers? Is this a likely accomplishment? What does Kino's fate suggest about Steinbeck's attitude toward this question?

4. OPPRESSION OF THE INDIANS

Mexico was conquered by the Spanish in the sixteenth century, and for generations, Mexican Indians were oppressed by people of Spanish descent. Steinbeck shows this oppression in his portrayal of the priest, the doctor, the pearl buyers, and the trackers. Steinbeck also comments on the relative worth of Indian and European-influenced civilization, suggesting in several places that the Indian culture in some respects may offer a happier environment for living than the "advanced" European culture.

5. MONEY AND POSSESSIONS

More than anything, Kino wants money so that he can pay for his son's education, purchase a rifle, and provide economic security for his family. But Kino never has the chance to find out if money buys happiness. Instead, he learns that the pearl is more of a curse than he can handle. The pearl, like an evil magnet, attracts a host of greedy people, and the only way for Kino to escape these people is to get rid of the object they seek. Kino discovers that wealth and good fortune are beyond his reach.

6. MAN AS PART OF NATURE

Steinbeck was fascinated by natural science. He had taken science courses at Stanford University, had worked in a fish hatchery, and was a good friend of Ed Ricketts, a marine biologist. While studying the shallow waters off the coast of Baja California, Steinbeck witnessed the war for survival among the various ocean species, as well as their many forms of interdependence. He saw striking similarities between human beings and other species.

When you read Chapters III and IV you'll notice Steinbeck's comparison of a town to a "colonial animal." Very primitive single-celled organisms (paramecia, for example) often group together into colonies—sometimes called aggregations—for the purpose of feeding or mating. Steinbeck used this biological aggregation as a model for the social groupings of higher level animals, including human beings. Human society is composed of individuals (like the single-celled animals), whose survival depends on interrelationships. Kino is alone when he finds the pearl, but the discovery of the pearl quickly travels throughout the village—the social, or colonial, animal—which reacts as an entirety with greed, envy, and dreams.

STYLE

The Pearl is a short novel. Its plot is well defined, the action moves forward within a structure of six chapters, it has a core of central characters, and the suspense builds as the story moves along. Readers say the sentences reflect the spoken quality of the New Testament—perhaps an influence of Steinbeck's early reading of the Bible. The author has chosen his words with precision, a skill he developed in part by working as a journalist.

In the preface to *The Pearl* you learn that the story will be told in the form of a parable. A parable is a short work, usually fictitious, that illustrates a lesson, often on the subject of good and evil. This is reminiscent of the New Testament, where many of Christ's lessons are told in parable form. The biblical tone is underscored by Steinbeck's mention in the preface of the struggle between good and evil.

Also, like the Bible (and traditional folktales), *The Pearl* contains little dialogue. The characters speak infrequently, but their thoughts and feelings are made clear through Steinbeck's powerful descriptions. He excelled at selecting the exact word and correct turn of phrase—and his lack of dialogue emphasizes the quiet intensity and simple manner of his characters. Their nonverbal quality helps to reinforce their discomfort in the presence of the sophisticated doctor, priest, and pearl buyers, who are experts at using language.

The Pearl contains many scientific metaphors and similes—figures of speech used to compare one object with another in order to suggest a similarity between them. For example, the Indian village is compared to the habitat of a colonial animal.

POINT OF VIEW

The Pearl is told by a third-person narrator who stands outside the action and knows everything about the characters and their actions. The narrator is said to be *omniscient*, which means all-knowing. In the introduction and in the final passage of the novel, the narrator speaks of events that happened long ago and have become important through repetition: "And because the story has been told so often, it has taken root in every man's mind."

For most of the novel, the narrator abandons the past and takes you directly into the present. This is the advantage of his omniscience: he can move back and forth, from past to present to future, whenever a different focus will help you understand his story. Perhaps the most gripping narrative in the present is the one where Kino attacks and kills the trackers. In this passage, you feel you are part of the action—as if you were standing next to Kino.

The movement from distant narration of the past to close-up narration that seems to recount the present may seem inconsistent. But remember that Steinbeck is trying to tell an old tale in the form of a novel. He needs a narrator who can communicate both the immediate action of the novel's plot and the universal nature of the tale (or parable).

The third-person narrative is also flexible in its focus on characters. It allows you to change perspectives and to judge the characters for their individual thoughts and actions. The thoughts and actions of characters are not filtered through the intelligence of one person, as in a first-person narration, but are presented reasonably objectively and with the wide-ranging facts available to an omniscient narrator.

FORM AND STRUCTURE

An important novel can usually be interpreted on many levels, and this is certainly the case with *The Pearl*. The book's structure is as simple as the legend, or folktale, on which it is based: It begins and ends with Kino as an impoverished fisherman who, in the process of pursuing his dream, is nearly destroyed. Readers often speak of *The Pearl* as an allegory or a parable.

An allegory is a story meant to teach a spiritual or moral lesson, in which the characters and action symbolize abstract concepts. A parable is a short allegory, which has long been associated with the New Testament. Christ used parables to teach moral lessons (for example, the Good Samaritan and the lesson of the Talents).

Some readers see *The Pearl* as an allegory of social oppression. In this view, Juan Tomás is a symbol of the ancient Indian wisdom, Kino is a symbol of the Indians' desire for freedom, and the doctor, priest, and pearl buyers are symbols of the oppressive Spanish culture. The pearl represents Kino's means of escaping oppression, but the powerful forces of the social system are too strong for even the pearl to overcome. When Kino throws his great treasure back into the sea, the message seems to be that the poor Indian doesn't have a chance.

Other readers see in *The Pearl* a strong allegorical message about human greed. Kino becomes the symbol of the poor but happy man who is destroyed when he begins to want the things of the material world. The pearl that was supposed to bring happiness and fulfillment brings only destruction. At the end both Kino's dream and his son are dead.

In the original story on which Steinbeck based his own, the fisher sees the pearl as a means of saving his soul through the purchase of Roman Catholic masses "sufficient to pop him out of Purgatory like a squeezed watermelon seed." (Purgatory, in Catholicism, is the temporary place or condition where the repentant sinner is absolved after death, and where mortal sins are punished before the soul can attain salvation.) When the fisher decides to throw the pearl back, he feels like a "free man" despite the insecurity of both his soul and his future.

In the novel, Kino says that the pearl has become his soul. This closely echoes the Gospel According to Matthew in the New Testament, in which the Kingdom of Heaven is compared to a "pearl of great price." If the pearl is seen as a symbol of salvation, what is the meaning of its loss at the end? Is Kino, like the fisherman of the original story, lucky to return to a state of simple human happiness and poverty? Or is he denied a soul as punishment for his reliance on material things, or for his daring to overreach his lowly status?

In his preface to *The Pearl*, Steinbeck says: "If the story is a parable, perhaps everyone takes his own meaning from it . . . ." It's up to you to decide whether the story is a parable, and what meaning you derive from it. In order to be effective, the true parable or allegory must attempt to resolve a conflict in such a way that a consistent interpretation or conclusion can be drawn. Do you think there is one such consistent meaning? Or, do you think the novel can be interpreted on many levels?

The Story
THE PREFACE

The Pearl begins with a short preface in which Steinbeck introduces the story of the great pearl, along with his three main characters—Kino the fisherman, his wife Juana, and their infant son Coyotito. Their story has been told so often, the Preface asserts, that it lives in people's minds and hearts. The story can be considered a parable.

NOTE: The introduction   Steinbeck inserted the Preface to make sure readers understood that the story had universal importance. Through stylized language and the suggestion of a parable, he indicates that you should look beyond the simple plot in order to find a deeper meaning. Perhaps

because he had been criticized for creating shallow
or flat characters, this short introduction is his way
of announcing that the characters are to be re-
garded mainly as symbols.

CHAPTER I

As a new day begins, Kino awakens peacefully
next to his sleeping wife. He is content with his
world and hears the Song of the Family playing
happily in his mind. It is an indication that all is
well.

NOTE: The songs and wholeness   Throughout *The
Pearl* you will read about various "songs" that play
in the minds of Steinbeck's characters. Such songs
include the Song of the Family and the Song of
Evil. These are ancient songs that have been passed
down by generations of Indians. Steinbeck uses
them to show the traditional, almost instinctual
responses of his characters to their environment.
When things are happy, they hear the Song of the
Family. When evil threatens, they are alerted by
the Song of Evil. Kino's songs often mark occasions of celebration: he celebrates the morning and
the existence of his family; he celebrates life and
its events. The songs were individual parts of the
Whole. This theme of wholeness is central to Steinbeck's thinking: everything has its place in the universe, and when something happens to one of the
parts, the whole system is affected.

Kino wraps himself in the one blanket that he owns, and watches the dawn break over the Gulf of California. The little Indian village is located somewhere on the peninsula of Baja California, Mexico, on the shore of the Gulf of California. While Juana prepares breakfast of corncake and pulque, Kino watches "with the detachment of God" as some ants try to outsmart each other in the dirt. His song blends with Juana's ancient song, and together they form a unity (the "Whole").

NOTE: The ants   From the very start, Steinbeck tries to show similarities between the human and animal worlds. The ants, sabotaging and outwitting each other with sand traps, are little different from human beings on the battlefield, in the marketplace, or in other human competitions. Notice that Kino does nothing to alter the outcome of the struggle. A major theme of *The Pearl* is man's struggle with nature and with the historical, racial, and class differences that prevent him from fulfilling his goals. By identifying Kino with God, is Steinbeck saying that man's life and struggles are not subject to divine interference? Try to keep some of these larger issues in mind as you read the novel.

Kino returns to his brush hut, a primitive abode with a crude doorway and mats on a dirt floor. A streak of sun falls on the rope that holds Coyotito's box. Suddenly, the peace of the morning is shattered when a scorpion crawls down the rope and stings the infant. Kino grabs the insect and grinds it into the dust while Juana takes her child and sucks out the poison. She whispers some ancient magic and mutters a "Hail Mary," which shows the Roman Catholic influence in her religious beliefs. Coyotito's screaming summons the neighbors, including Kino's older brother, Juan Tomás, and his fat wife, Apolonia. Kino watches Juana in action and wonders at her strength, endurance, and patience.

NOTE: The scorpion episode The scorpion attack is part of the human struggle for existence and parallels the attacks by men later on. Steinbeck uses this attack to point out the difficulty of life in general—that no matter how hard people struggle in life, there always seems to be another problem or obstacle in their path.

Juana tells Kino to get the doctor. While this may seem like a reasonable request, it is actually an unusual one for an Indian. The class distinctions between the poor Indians and people of Spanish descent like the doctor were enormous. Kino realizes that since he is an Indian and has no money, the doctor will not come to treat Coyotito. Hearing that, Juana decides they will go to him. The theme of wholeness arises again when the villagers swarm around Juana and Kino: "The thing had become a neighborhood affair." As mentioned earlier, the Whole is affected when something happens to one of the parts.

NOTE: Class distinctions Hundreds of years ago, Spanish conquerors took over Mexico and established their social, political, and economic dominance over the Indian population. The Spaniards and their descendants, because of their money and military power, became the ruling class. The Indians became the exploited, lower class.

The villagers, amazed by this decision, follow Juana and Kino to the doctor's house, passing the four beggars who gather in front of the church. Steinbeck uses the beggars to illustrate the doctor's character: "They knew his ignorance, his cruelty, his avarice, his appetites, his sins. They knew his clumsy abortions and the little brown pennies he gave sparingly for alms." Through this unspoken knowledge about the doctor, you come to see the class struggle that is part of the lives of the members of Kino's tribe.

Everyone suspects the doctor will not treat Coyotito. But the parents must try anyway. In his rage, Kino pounds against the doctor's gate with the iron ring knocker. His thoughts about the doctor are described in the language of oppression: weakness, fear, anger, rage, and terror. The pounding of the music of the enemy mixes with the sound of the iron ring pounding at the doctor's gate.

The servant who answers the call is an Indian like Kino, yet he will not speak to Kino in his own language. He makes it clear that Kino must wait for an answer outside the bolted gate.

NOTE: On language Language is used here as a sign of class distinction. When the Indian servant

says, "A little moment," Steinbeck is implying that
he is speaking Spanish—*un momentito*. The *-ito*
ending gives a noun the meaning of "small" or
"tiny." The baby's name, Coyotito, means "a little
coyote." When the servant refuses to speak in the
Indian language, he is reminding Kino of his lowly
place. The incident also shows that people of
Spanish descent set Indians against each other.

The doctor's home, elegantly decadent, represents "the other world" and is contrasted with the
primitive Indian huts. The doctor, dressed in a silk
dressing gown (robe) that barely covers his fat belly,
sips chocolate clumsily from a delicate china cup.
He has the trappings of the rich, whereas you have
seen that Kino eats corncake in the dirt, near a fire,
wrapped in an old blanket. By now, you have
probably noticed the tone of a parable, which is
designed to teach a simple moral lesson. What
message is Steinbeck communicating in this contrast between the doctor and the Indians?

As expected, the doctor, claiming that he is not
a veterinarian, refuses to treat Coyotito. A wave
of shame engulfs the people who witness Kino's
humiliation. Kino stands at the gate for a long time,
then angrily punches it. He stares at his bloody
knuckles, a symbol of the struggle between people
of Spanish background and Indians. The doctor's
insulting refusal shocks Kino into realizing that
something drastic must happen if he is to provide
for his son's future. It's not that Kino or his family
must "change," but that they must find some way
of exerting control over their environment. Do you

think that Kino is a victim of fate? Are there changes
he could have made to improve his life?

NOTE: Nature vs. civilization   Steinbeck uses
nature imagery to contrast the Indians with the
"civilized" life of the town. The doctor, who represents those who control the village, lives in a
large home of stone and plaster, while Kino and
the other Indians live in an impoverished neighborhood of small brush huts with dirt floors.
Whereas the doctor drinks chocolate from a sil-
ver pot, Kino drinks pulque (a fermented drink
made from a flowering plant) from an earthen jug,
squatting on the dirt. The doctor sleeps in a plush
bed, but Kino and his wife sleep on simple mats
thrown on the ground. Yet the doctor's house is
gloomy and dark, whereas Kino's hut is right on
the beautiful Gulf of California. The doctor is
frustrated and greedy; Kino is happy and content. The doctor has money; Kino has none. The
doctor is agitated; the Indians are in tune with
nature. The doctor is "refined"; the Indians have
the simple, instinctual ways of animals. ("All the
doctor's race spoke to all of Kino's race as though
they were simple animals.")

What does this contrast tell you? One idea to
think about is that the further one moves away
from nature, the more "unnatural" one becomes.
And with this move toward a culture based on
money, one grows more discontent with life, more
restricted and tense. The birds at the Gulf fly free,
while the doctor's bird is caged. Kino is at peace
when the novel begins. But he is soon thrown into
conflict when he leaves nature in pursuit of money

and civilization. This conflict will persist until he
returns to his natural habitat.

CHAPTER II

In the opening description of the beach, the narrator leads your eyes inland from the sea. The beach
and the water nearby are full of life, each creature
living and growing in its own way and in its own
place. Despite the vision of the sea teeming with
life, the narrator cautions that in the Gulf, vision
cannot be trusted. The hazy mirages that occur
there have taught Kino's people for centuries not
to trust their vision, for the Gulf has "the vague-
ness of a dream."

Kino's village is located on a broad estuary lined
with canoes. He and Juana are proud of his canoe—
a gift from his father, who had received it from
Kino's grandfather. It is their only possession of
value and symbolizes the ancient Indian civilization that continues to guide Kino. As his source of
income, the canoe is a necessity.

That morning, when Kino and Juana come down
to the beach, she makes a poultice (medicinal com-
press) of seaweed for Coyotito's shoulder. This is
probably a better remedy than what the doctor
would have offered, yet it lacks the doctor's authority. Worrying about her son, Juana prays that
they will find a pearl in order to pay the doctor to
heal Coyotito.

NOTE: Juana's natural instincts are strong. She
reacts to the situations in her life with compassion

and intelligence, as her administering of her poultice demonstrates. But she is aware of her simplicity and doubts the effectiveness of her methods, when compared with those of the doctor. Keep this in mind when you read of the doctor's actions in the next chapter.

After pushing the canoe into the water, Kino and Juana work together to paddle toward the oyster bed where Kino fishes and searches for pearls. The oyster bed has historical significance. Steinbeck notes that the Spanish conquerors had worked this bed and that the pearls taken from it had greatly aided the king of Spain, financing both his wars and the decoration of his churches.

NOTE: Pearl formation   Pearls are formed through an accident of nature. A grain of sand becomes caught inside the fleshy folds of an oyster and, to protect itself from irritation, the oyster coats the grain with layer after layer of a milky cement. This process forms a pearl. This contrast between the natural definition of a pearl and its value to humans in terms of wealth is one of the many contrasts Steinbeck uses to tell you something significant about reality and appearances. It is also one of the many levels of symbolic meaning that the pearl conveys.

Kino knows that a great pearl will bring him much money, but he does not dare hope for such a pearl because it is not good to want too much.

As he descends into the water, he hears the Song
of the Pearl That Might Be, and in the canoe above,
Juana makes the "magic of prayer."

Moments after Kino goes underwater, he finds
a large oyster in which there is a "ghostly gleam."
It is the Pearl of the World—great and perfect and
stunning. Kino's troubles seem to be over. The
money he will receive from the sale of the pearl
will eliminate the humiliations of poverty. Yet Kino
does not hope for too much since that might drive
good luck away. Kino's people have always felt a
need to be tactful with both the Christian God and
the old Indian gods so as not to appear greedy.
Why do you think they feel this way?

NOTE: Superstitions   Juana and Kino do not want
to offend the gods by hoping for too much. On
one level this is a superstition inherited from their
ancestors (Juana's "magic of prayer"). But on another level, it is consistent with the idea of wholeness, whereby each person plays his part in life
and removes from life what is his due. Though
illiterate, Juana and Kino understand the principle
of balance. If you ask for more than your fair share,
you may end up with even less. Notice that the
pearl gives off a "ghostly gleam." Already there is
a hint of death.

Kino looks at the pearl and sees that it captures
the light as perfectly as the moon. He can see
dreams of a better future for his family in the pearl.
This passage marks the beginning of Kino's dreams,
or "visions," where reality becomes confused with

the illusion of a better world. His dreams go deep—right through to his soul—and Kino will soon begin to identify his soul with the pearl. Don't forget the warning about mirages, however, at the beginning of the chapter. Will the pearl prove a lucky find or something quite different?

While Kino holds the pearl in the hand he had smashed against the doctor's gate, Juana notices that Coyotito's swelling has gone down. The poison is leaving the infant's body. Kino screams with delight as he looks at the pearl, and this causes the other divers to race toward his canoe.

By screaming so loudly, Kino attracts attention to his discovery. This sets in motion the reactions of the community, each person adding to the total reaction of the whole. Before he knows it, Kino will become alienated from the people of his own village. He will be the outsider who deviates from the natural system. And in biological systems, the deviant is usually punished, sometimes by death. If you were in Kino's shoes, would you react as he did?

CHAPTER III

Kino's village is compared to a "colonial animal," with a physical body, emotions, and a nervous system that communicates news in a rapid, invisible way. By the time Kino and Juana return to their house, everyone knows that he has found the Pearl of the World. Suddenly, people become interested in Kino. When the priest hears the news, he thinks of certain repairs needed by the church. The doctor, fantasizing about his younger, happier days in Paris, announces that Kino is his client and that he is treating Coyotito for the scorpion sting.

NOTE: Theme of wholeness With the comparison of the village to a colonial animal, Steinbeck presents his idea that each person is part of a larger whole. No event happens to an individual in isolation. The procession of villagers to the doctor's house prepared you for this idea. And it is reinforced by the closeness felt by Mexican Indians to their village. There is a feeling of belonging, perhaps because of village unity and the hierarchy of power. Rarely do people leave their village.

The unscrupulous pearl buyers are delighted by the news. Though they pretend to be independent buyers with private little offices, they all work for the same man. They are the "arms" of his organization, and nothing gives them more pleasure than buying pearls at ridiculously low prices.

A "curiously dark residue" is created when the people think about Kino's pearl. It taps into their dreams, plans, hopes, fantasies, and desires. And the only person preventing them from fulfilling their dreams is Kino. Because of this, he becomes every man's enemy, though he doesn't know it. His discovery has provoked something thoroughly evil in the town, a "black distillate" as poisonous as the scorpion. This comparison of the pearl's effect with the scorpion's poison is one of the major biological comparisons in *The Pearl*. (Another is the description of the village as a colonial animal.) The pearl, once a source of promise and beauty, has now become an evil omen.

NOTE: Greed and envy   The pearl causes a sinister change in town. Kino has become a "have" in a world of "have-nots." As a result, he is an outsider, an enemy. The pearl has planted the seeds of many dreams in the minds of many people who have been deprived of too much for too long. Their greed and envy create a threat to Kino. In his excitement, Kino is blinded to events around him. But his brother, Juan Tomás, sees the threat and will warn Kino about it.

Later, Kino sits with his family and friends, admiring the pearl. Juan Tomás asks what he will do now that he has become rich. Kino peers into the pearl for an answer, as if looking into a crystal ball. He has a vision of a proper church wedding, where he and Juana will be dressed in fine clothes. And he will purchase a harpoon and a rifle.

Kino wants status and recognition, and it is the rifle that seems to symbolically break down the social order that keeps the Indians under the domination of the Spaniards. While it is acceptable for Kino to imagine having a wedding, fine clothes, and other niceties, a rifle would ordinarily be an impossible purchase for poor Indians. The mere thought of Kino's owning a rifle tells you that he has crossed the line that separates his original simple life from the passion for wealth that will devour him. The rifle symbolizes Kino's intention to cease being exploited by people of Spanish descent. In the hands of an Indian, a gun could change the power structure. So could the next part of Kino's dream—an education for his son—since knowledge will eventually free the Indians from the bonds of ignorance. Qn an even higher symbolic level, the rifle might be thought of as the final blow of truth that allows innocence and goodness to triumph over evil. This passage about Kino's visions reminds you that *The Pearl* is an allegory in which concrete objects often stand for ideas.

At dusk, the villagers whisper that the priest is coming. Like the doctor, the priest lives in town and rarely visits these "children." Without knowing why, Kino hears the Song of Evil, but faintly, when the priest enters. The Father says Kino is named for a great man of the Church (Eusebio Kino, a Jesuit missionary in present-day Mexico and Arizona from the 1680s to his death in 1711) and that it is in the books. Kino isn't sure of this and hopes that someday his son will know what is in the books. The priest wants to make certain that the Church gets its share from the sale of the pearl. Do you think Steinbeck is implying that the Church contributes to the exploitation of the Indians?

NOTE: Kino, the priest, and religion The priest's visit is preceded by the suggestion that Kino might be punished for trying to change things. How are God, the priest, the future, and Kino's plans related? Kino believes that his future is vulnerable to attack because he has spoken openly of his plans. In fact, Kino feels threatened by this representative of religion. Although the priest appears to be concerned that Kino do the "right" thing, his major interest is the pearl. His stilted biblical language ("thou" and "thee") rings false. And he has not married Kino in the church or baptized Coyotito because Kino has never had the money to pay for these services. Do you think the priest's actions are motivated by self-interest? Remember that in the original story Kino wants to use the pearl's wealth primarily to guarantee his salvation by purchasing in advance the masses necessary to release his soul from Purgatory. Doesn't such a practice as buying one's salvation also suggest the corruption of the Church?

After the priest leaves, Kino still hears the shrill music of evil in his ears. A thin dog wanders by, but as Kino looks down, he fails to see the animal. This is another sign that Kino's eyes are blind to simple, everyday events.

The doctor arrives after dark. Kino is filled with hatred, rage, and fear, but lets the doctor in when the corrupt old man says there might be a delayed reaction to the scorpion sting. In his ignorance, Kino does not know what to do, but he does not want his son to suffer.

To play on the couple's fears, the doctor puts on a grand show. He gives the baby some poisonous white powder and says he will come back in an hour, for he knows the poison will strike by then. When the doctor leaves, Kino buries the pearl in the corner of the hut. Coyotito becomes very sick again, and in an hour the doctor returns.

NOTE: Before the doctor returns, Steinbeck inserts an important description of the estuary at night. There is the sound of big fish eating little fish, the familiar sound of slaughter—a symbol of the relationship between the Spanish and the Indians, between the rulers and the oppressed.

The doctor has not fooled anyone, even though he gives Coyotito a few drops of ammonia in a cup of water to calm him. The doctor says that because of his knowledge of scorpion poison, Coyotito will now recover. He pretends to be surprised that Kino has found a pearl, but asks questions, hoping that Kino will glance at the place where the pearl is hidden. Kino does this, and the doctor leaves the hut knowing the location of the pearl.

Later that night, Kino and Juana are awakened by an intruder in their hut. Fearing this might happen, Kino had moved the pearl. But he is wounded in the scuffle with the attacker.

For the first time, Juana begs Kino to get rid of the pearl. She feels it is evil and will destroy them. But Kino resists. He is infatuated with dreams of the future and refuses to surrender to outsiders.

NOTE: The shrewd and conniving doctor is one of the first to prey upon Kino, but he will not be the last. Juana's instincts about the pearl are correct, and Kino's stubbornness will launch him on a path of destruction. Within the scope of the parable, what does Kino's attitude tell you about the quest for money? Whose side do you take in the disagreement between Juana and Kino?

CHAPTER IV

This is the day Kino will sell the pearl. Everyone in La Paz is aware of Kino's plans and will take part in the ritual. Juana wears her wedding skirt and dresses Coyotito in baptismal clothes. Kino steps out of his hut and heads up the procession, accompanied by his brother, Juan Tomás. Though Juana walks behind her husband, there will be a time when she breaks custom and walks together with him.

Juan Tomás warns Kino to beware of the pearl buyers. They are cheats, he says, and will try to fool him about the price. He reminds Kino of the time some men in the village wanted to obtain more money for their pearls by pooling them and sending an Indian agent to the capital to sell them. Twice they tried it, but on both occasions the agents disappeared. Do you think the agents ran off with the money, or were they perhaps robbed and killed?

The brothers talk about the annual sermon that the priest delivers on this incident. He insists it's a message from God that each person is meant to maintain his or her position in life, whatever it might be: "Each man and woman is like a soldier sent by God to guard some part of the castle of the Universe."

NOTE: When you consider the source of this sermon—the priest—you may conclude that it's a story he uses to manipulate the Indians. There is a strong political and social component—God wants you to stay in your place—and the Indians are expected to obey. It is very possible that Steinbeck wants you to regard the sermon in the same light as the doctor's remedies. Do you think Kino and Juan Tomás believe the priest's message?

The brothers squint their eyes and tighten their lips in preparation for the pearl buyers. The people in the procession know that this is an important day, and they follow Kino's lead.

In the meantime, the pearl buyers sit at their desks, excited about the much-discussed pearl. One of them, a fat, plodding man, plays disappearing tricks with a coin while waiting. The symbolic disappearance of the coin foreshadows the episode that follows.

When Kino arrives, the villagers wait outside while he shows one of the buyers his pearl. The pearl buyers have already conspired how to handle the buying of the pearl. With a look of sadness and contempt for the poor man who doesn't know the value of things, one of the buyers tells Kino that the pearl, like fool's gold, is only a curiosity. He offers Kino a thousand pesos, but Kino knows it is worth fifty thousand.

Kino, growing "tight and hard," feels the circling of vultures and wolves. He hears the music of the enemy and knows that he is being cheated. As if to confirm his price, the pearl buyer sends for the other buyers, claiming that they know nothing of his offer. The first man refuses to do business because the pearl is a "monstrosity." The second dealer says it is soft, chalky, and worthless. The third offers five hundred pesos.

Disgusted, Kino withdraws his pearl and says he'll sell it in the capital. The men, realizing they have not fooled Kino, promptly offer fifteen hundred pesos. They know that they will be punished by their boss if they don't purchase the pearl. But Kino understands their scheme and decides to leave.

That evening, the villagers discuss Kino's decision. Some support him; others think he was wrong. Kino, however, is terrified of what he has done. He feels he has "lost one world and [has] not gained another." What do you think this means? Kino knows more about the world than he did a few days earlier. Though he is vulnerable, he must harden himself to the attacks that await him. His instinctual awareness of this causes him anxiety, as does the idea of leaving the village of his birth.

Juan Tomás sees that Kino is treading on new ground without knowing the way. He says that, in the capital, Kino will be among strangers and will be leaving behind his friends and family. (If you have been looking for the symbolic meaning of the characters, look carefully at Juan Tomás here. Do you see why some readers think he represents the traditional Indian ways?) Only Juana seems to be on Kino's side, even though the pearl frightens her.

Later on, Kino is restless and goes for a walk. Sensing danger, he feels for his knife. Juana hears a scuffle and puts the baby down to look for a rock in order to come to Kino's aid. By the time she reaches Kino, his clothes have been torn apart by an attacker looking for the pearl. He is half conscious, his cheek slashed.

Juana cleans the wound, then pleads with Kino to throw the pearl away. Kino can only repeat his dream, as if repetition will make it come true. He asks Juana to believe in him ("I am a man"), then promises they will leave for the capital in the morning.

NOTE: You might be wondering about the relationship between Kino and Juana at this point. It is clear that Kino has deep love and respect for his wife. She is warm and loving and also strong and secure. Yet within the social structure of their society, the male is the absolute head of the family. Do you think Kino is comfortable as the decision maker? Or would he prefer to share responsibility equally with Juana? He seems obsessed with his dream and, for the moment, won't let anyone, including Juana, challenge it.

CHAPTER V

Kino awakens in the darkness as Juana quietly leaves the hut with something in her hand. Enraged, Kino follows her to the shore. But when she sees him coming, Juana begins to run. Kino grabs her arm before she can throw the pearl into the water. Then, hissing like a snake, he beats her. When she falls against the rocks, he kicks her viciously in the side. This is the same Kino who had so tenderly loved her two days earlier and had wondered at her strength.

What has changed him? What makes them both do what they are doing? Juana wants to expose the dream-filled destruction she sees Kino driven toward. But she doesn't fight back, because submission is part of her role as Kino's wife. When

Kino beats her, he is defending his manliness and his dream, for the two have become one.

NOTE: Kino's dream Kino's dream has challenged the system. In Chapter IV, Steinbeck showed you the reflexive response of the town, the colonial animal, to the pearl. In the deepening conflict, Kino will lose everything that connects him to this town. The purpose of Chapter V is to show Kino's isolation. If you keep in mind the metaphor (comparison) of the town as a colonial animal, this separation can mean only one thing—destruction. Kino's battle with Juana foreshadows the death of his family. He is now like the deviant from a closely interrelated ecological system. He is separated from his natural environment. From now on, he will lack the protection of his kin and the strength of his tradition. He is a free agent, flung into the world to face ruthless predators.

Kino is attacked again on the path to his hut— this time, by more than one assailant. In self-defense, Kino kills one of them, and with this action, Juana realizes that their old way of life is ended. She finds the pearl in the path just before seeing the two men lying there, one of whom is bleeding from the throat. She sponges Kino's wounds and revives him after dragging the dead man into the bushes. As Kino recovers consciousness, she tells him what has happened, and they realize they must leave the village before daybreak.

By killing a man, Kino has crossed a threshold; there is now no turning back to the old life. Before this, Kino could have sold the pearl and given up his dream of changing the way things are. In his quest for his dream, Kino rebels against both the natural and the social systems—and tries to impose his own will. This attempted revolt will bring Kino ever closer to destruction.

Kino instructs Juana to prepare Coyotito and pack some food while he readies the canoe. As he stumbles down to the beach, he is horrified to see that his canoe has been destroyed.

NOTE: The canoe   For Kino, as for any fisherman, the destruction of his boat is an immeasurable loss. Not only does it mean the loss of his prized possession and his means to an income, but it also means the loss of a part of his heritage. The psychological impact of the loss of his canoe is as significant for Kino as the dead man in the path was for Juana. The old way of life is over. Filled with rage, Kino now becomes like an animal, living only to protect himself and his family. (But notice that even in his rage, it never occurs to Kino to take another's boat.) Why does Steinbeck use this animal comparison? Does Kino really have to become like an animal to preserve his dream of a better life as a man? Is Steinbeck necessarily implying that animal traits are lower than human ones?

Juana scurries down the path with the news that their hut is on fire. She and Kino make plans to hide in his brother's house until the next night, when they will leave for the mountains. Juan Tomás tells him that there is a devil in the pearl, but he agrees to help Kino. He spends the day telling neighbors that Kino has fled the village. From each visit, he returns with something borrowed that will help his brother—a few beans, some salt, and a knife.

That night, before the moon rises, Kino sets forth with his family. Once more, Juan Tomás asks Kino to consider giving up the pearl. But Kino answers that the pearl has become his soul, and that if he gives it up, he will lose his soul.

NOTE: The pearl as Kino's soul   Kino has become so obsessed with the pearl that nothing else matters. Every breath is devoted to making his dream come true, at the risk of placing his family in grave danger. In a material sense, a person dies when his soul leaves his body. If Kino were to throw away his soul, he would die spiritually as well. His soul—that is, the pearl and his dream— is all that holds him to life. Why do you think Kino considers the pearl as his soul? Do you see a religious meaning here? Has Kino substituted a dream of fulfillment on earth for the traditional Christian concept of salvation after death? Some readers think that the dream of the pearl has corrupted Kino's true soul, driving him to sacrifice his family and reject his past. Others see the pearl as Kino's only hope for dignity as a man. In this sense, the pearl would be a fitting metaphor for his soul.

CHAPTER VI

The moment has come for Kino and his family to leave their village in search of their dream. This

chapter can best be understood when divided into
three parts: the flight, the confrontation with the
trackers, and the return.

Kino and Juana flee toward Loreto, the city where
"the miraculous Virgin has her station." They make
certain, however, not to be seen in the town of La
Paz where, two days earlier, they had led a procession to the doctor's house. There is a strong wind
this night as the couple go "out into the world."
(These words may remind you of Adam and Eve
leaving the Garden of Eden in the Old Testament
Book of Genesis.) Kino is grateful for the wind
because it means the blowing sand will cover their
tracks.

The flight has stirred something primitive and
basic in Kino, as if part of his ancient Indian heritage has reawakened in him. His survival instinct
(akin to animal instinct) has been revived, and he
is wary of attackers.

Hour after hour the march proceeds until at last
they come upon a road with deeply cut wheel tracks.
Since the wind has died down, they decide to walk
in the tracks as an added safety measure. A wagon
cutting through the sand will easily erase their foot-
steps. Though the evils of the night are all around
them, Kino hears the music of the pearl in his head.
The screeching owls and laughing coyotes do not
trouble him, since he has the knife for protection.

NOTE: Kino and Juana's march to Loreto resem-
bles a pilgrimage to a religious shrine. In fact,
Steinbeck notes that Loreto is the city where the
Virgin Mary "has her station." Kino's passion for
the pearl approaches an almost religious fervor.

You've seen earlier that Kino and Juana combine
ancient Indian and Catholic prayers, that they re-
fer to God and the gods. Has the religion of the
pearl taken over from both these sets of belief?
Have all Kino's gods abandoned him, or is it the
other way around?

At dawn, after walking all night, they find a little
hiding spot in a clearing near the road. Juana set-
tles in to feed Coyotito while Kino returns to the
road to sweep away their footprints. Before long,
a cart creeks along the path, wiping out all the
tracks. Relieved, Kino returns to Juana and shares
some corncakes with her. While eating, Kino spots
a little column of ants near his foot; he puts his
foot in their way and watches them climb over it.
Recall that in Chapter I, Kino did not interfere with
the ants, despite his God-like position. Now he
makes the ants climb over his foot, a difficult task
for an ant. Is Steinbeck commenting on God's in-
difference to human struggle? Would God create
an obstacle as carelessly as Kino puts his foot in
the ants' path?

It is hot and they are far from the Gulf. Kino
shows Juana the poisonous trees and bushes to
avoid. In the midst of these warnings, Juana asks
if they are being followed. Kino knows that this
will happen and that it will prove the pearl's worth.
He looks into the pearl for his former vision of the
future but sees only pictures of the past—the dead
man, Juana's beaten face, and the baby's illness.
In an effort to blot out these images, Kino asserts
that their son will have a fine education. Yet all he
sees is Coyotito's face, "thick and feverish from

medicine." Alarmed by the vision, Kino hears the music of evil intermingled with that of the pearl.

NOTE: Kino's visions Throughout the novel, Kino has seen visions in the pearl. In keeping with a cinematic technique, Steinbeck has used the pearl as a sort of mirror in which Kino sees visual reflections of his mind. When he is excited about the future, the vision shows his church wedding, fine clothes, and Coyotito going to school. Now that he is a pursued animal, Kino's visions show only the dark, frightening aspects of life. What role do these visions play on the symbolic level of the story?

Kino falls asleep. Steinbeck then describes the impassive Juana, sitting with the flies buzzing around her facial cuts and bruises, watching Coyotito until his innocent playing makes her smile and respond.

The two of them together make clear the difficulty of their own and their people's position. The Indians have little choice. If they submit meekly to oppression, they will be allowed to live as we see Juana living. They will be beaten any time they try to change things. But they will also be allowed a measure of innocent contentment as long as they do not peer into the future. (Do you remember how happy Kino was on that first morning? Juana is also happy watching the innocence of the baby.) If they do not submit, they will be crushed.

Kino sits up suddenly and whispers to Juana to be silent. He hears something and feels for his knife. In the distance, he sees two men on foot and one on horseback. They are trackers in search of the pearl, and Kino knows they will persist until they find him. He fears that careless footprints will reveal his whereabouts and that even his sweeping the footprints might give him away. Kino is now a hunted man.

NOTE: Steinbeck is a master of suspense. One of his strengths as a novelist is the ability to keep the story moving. Even with its many descriptions, *The Pearl* maintains a rapid pace. As it moves to a conclusion, you can almost feel Kino and Juana running.

As the trackers approach, Kino plans to leap at the one with the rifle, then kill the other two. Juana muffles Coyotito's noises while the trackers stop at the swept spot. After closely examining the sand, the trackers move on, look back, then continue their journey. Kino knows that they will return, and he panics like a trapped animal. Flight is the only solution. Finally, Juana provokes him into making a decision: they will go to the mountains.

They hurry frantically toward the high place, not bothering to cover their tracks. Time is crucial since the trackers will soon discover the broken twigs and crushed plants. Kino wants Juana to remain in the crevice while he plants false signs that will lead the trackers further up into the mountains. But she refuses to leave him. So they decide to move in zigzags instead of a straight line, leaving a multitude of signs to confuse the trackers.

The flight to the mountains suggests several

meanings. One is that Kino's action is a natural one. "And Kino ran for the high place, as nearly all animals do when they are pursued." Another level of meaning comes from the image of the "naked granite mountains . . . standing monolithic against the sky." The image is a reminder of the implacable forces of both nature and society against which the Indians must struggle to survive. Some readers find a reference to another, older story of a father who takes his son to the mountains. They see the story of Kino and Coyotito as a reversal of the Old Testament story of Abraham and Isaac. (See Note on page 50.)

As the sun falls, they climb higher to a bubbling spring where animals come to drink. Kino knows that the trackers, needing water, will also plan to come here. But that's a risk he'll have to take. From this altitude, Kino spots the trackers far down the slope. They appear no bigger than swarming ants.

NOTE: Ant imagery   This is the third time that ants have appeared in *The Pearl*. Steinbeck uses them to show the parallels between animal and human behavior, and to portray the relative insignificance of individual human beings in the scheme of the universe.

Juana takes a supply of water and heads for a cave up above. Meanwhile, Kino runs up the mountain, then down again, "clawing and tearing at the ferns and wild grape" as he goes. By misleading the trackers into climbing higher, he and Juana will be able to escape down the mountain.

His one fear is that Coyotito's cries will reveal their location. But Juana says this won't happen.

By dusk, the trackers arrive at the water spring. Kino watches them from the cave entrance and realizes that they intend to set up camp. This is bad news since he and Juana know they won't be able to keep Coyotito quiet for the entire night. Kino has no choice but to kill the trackers.

Kino touches his son on the head, then feels Juana's cheek. In preparation for the murder, Kino strips the last remains of civilization—his clothes— from his body. Kino's naked, brown body now camouflages him. He must move slowly in order not to dislodge a stone. This requires great stamina—the courage of an animal on the prowl. As Kino reaches the trackers' camp, his heart thunders as he prepares for the attack.

Just as Kino is about to strike, the moon makes him very visible. He hesitates for a moment—a tragic mistake—and the baby cries, drawing the attention of the tracker on duty. In a bitter play on the baby's name, the trackers discuss whether it is a human cry or that of a coyote with her litter. The man with the rifle, taking no chances, raises the rifle to shoot. Kino springs, but he is a moment too late. The rifle goes off before Kino reaches him.

NOTE: Abraham and Isaac   Some readers see the fate of Coyotito in the mountains as a reminder of the biblical story of Abraham and Isaac—in reverse. In that story, Abraham was instructed by God to take his son to the mountain and sacrifice him. When Abraham showed God that he was willing to make the sacrifice, God substituted a ram for Isaac and rewarded Abraham. "I will indeed bless you, and I will multiply your descendants as the stars of heaven and as the sand which is on the seashore. And your descendants shall possess the gate of their enemies . . . . "(Genesis 22: 15–18) In *The Pearl*, the son is sacrificed; God has not interceded. And there seems little chance of Kino's descendants overcoming their enemies. Unlike Abraham, however, Kino is denied the chance to save his people.

In a frenzy of rage, Kino takes on a machinelike quality and kills all three trackers—one with his knife, one with a blow to the head with the rifle butt, and one slowly and deliberately with shots from the rifle. After the sounds of the killing fade away, Kino hears mournful sounds. It is Juana— something terrible has happened to Coyotito. His head has been blown away.

Steinbeck ends the chapter with a description of the sad return of Kino and Juana to their native village. Not only do the old people who actually saw them return remember it, but also the younger ones whose fathers and grandfathers told them about it. The event truly involved everyone in the village of La Paz.

It is late afternoon when the couple returns to La Paz (ironically, La Paz is Spanish for peace). Walking side by side, Kino carries the rifle and Juana supports Coyotito's body in a bundle over her shoulder. Juana is "as remote and as removed as Heaven," while Kino is "as dangerous as a rising storm."

NOTE: You will recall that, earlier in *The Pearl*, Juana walked behind her husband. Now they walk together, side by side. What do you see in this new sign of equality? Is it an indication that they are now removed from the old system that has oppressed them? Or is it a sign that they are no longer a part of their ancient Indian culture?

Kino and Juana walk through the town as if it weren't there. Passing the ruins of their burned hut, they proceed to the water, where Kino takes the pearl, looks into it, and sees evil faces peering at him. The pearl has become ugly, "like a malignant growth." Kino asks if Juana wants to throw it, but she tells him to do it. With that, he flings it into the Gulf, where it splashes in the distance, then drops to the bottom, its music fading away to nothing.

NOTE: Some conclusions It is bitter irony that after all Kino suffers to keep the pearl, he throws it back into the ocean, where it is lost forever. How can we understand why Kino does this and what the meanings of this story of the poor fisherman might be?

Does Kino throw the pearl away because he feels guilty, as some readers suggest? If this is so, then Kino must feel that he has been greedy and that his greed has caused the death of Coyotito, all the other deaths, and much pain and suffering. The original version of the legend was clearly a warning about greed. Can you see a parallel warning in Kino's final gesture?

We know there is rage in Kino at the end, because Steinbeck uses images like "a rising storm," "a tower of fear," and "a battle cry" in his description of Kino's return. Do you think Kino throws the pearl away as a gesture of rage and disgust? Has he learned that Indians are not allowed to dream? Is the gesture a last protest against social oppression?

You might also conclude that Kino's new understanding stretches even further than the boundaries of his own social system. It was not only the pearl buyers and the doctor and the tracker with the horse who betrayed him. Indians also worked against him. (He had to beg his brother for one day's refuge!) It is possible that Kino at the end looks with disgust at humans in general, regardless of social position. From this point of view, the novel seems to be a depiction of the universal weakness and selfishness of people.

Still another conclusion is that Kino's tragedy was not so much a victory of evil over good as it was a natural phenomenon. Throughout the novel, Steinbeck has used biological comparisons to suggest that no event happens to an individual alone. The natural order—of ants, fish, scorpions, and men—is a predatory one, and Kino just happens to get caught in it. Kino's action might suggest that he is submitting to the inevitability of the natural (and social) order—to his fate.

There is no single answer. The meaning you take from this story of the fisherman and the pearl will depend on how you see Kino and on how you interpret the meaning of the pearl, on your own experiences, and on many other factors. Steinbeck does not point dramatically and conclusively to one interpretation. Some readers have seen this inconclusiveness as a weakness in the novel. Perhaps *The Pearl* is not conclusive, but it does serve as a kind of record of the conflicts experienced by people—conflicts within themselves and with the systems under which they live.

A STEP BEYOND

Tests and Answers
TESTS

Test 1

1. The songs in *The Pearl* represent _____
   A. unspoken feelings and emotions
   B. domination by the Spanish
   C. the poetry Kino has inherited from his ancestors

2. Which of the following similes does _____ Steinbeck use to describe the relationship of the townspeople?
   A. Each man's life is like a station in God's army.
   B. The pearl is like a curse.
   C. The town is like a colonial animal.

3. After finding the pearl in the path, Juana _____ didn't throw it back in the water because
   A. she was afraid of getting hit again
   B. Kino stopped her again
   C. she knew the old way was gone when she saw the dead man

4. Before Kino finds the pearl, his life might _____ be described as
   A. filled with want and despair
   B. simple and relatively content
   C. monotonous and uncomfortable

5. The image of big fish eating little fish is _____ symbolic of the relationship between the

    A. Spanish and the Indians
    B. pearl buyers and their unseen boss
    C. trackers and Kino

6. Which of the following religious references   _____
   is *not* appropriate to *The Pearl*?
    A. the Abraham and Isaac story
    B. the miracle of the loaves and the
       fishes
    C. the expulsion from the Garden of
       Eden

7. When Kino punches the doctor's gate, you   _____
   can tell he
    A. has planned the action of protest from
       the beginning
    B. has been provoked to this kind of
       violent expression before
    C. surprises himself with the violence of
       his reaction

8. In the story of the two villagers who had   _____
   gone to the capital to sell pearls, it was certain that they had
    A. fled with the profits
    B. been in the employ of the Spanish
    C. never been seen again

9. The doctor's actions are meant to suggest   _____
   that
    A. this is the way the Spanish generally
       treat the Indians
    B. he is incompetent and has no
       business treating the baby
    C. he is different from the other Spanish

10. Which of the following is *not* true about   _____
    Kino's canoe?

    A. It was passed down to him from his
       grandfather.
    B. It had been blessed by the priest.
    C. It was the one thing of value owned
       by Kino.

11. Why is Kino's dream of educating Coyotito such a dangerous one?

12. What role does Juan Tomás play?

13. Explain the symbolism of the pearl.

Test 2

1. When Kino said, "I am a man," Juana knew   _____
   this meant that he
   A. no longer needed her
   B. would leave the old way of life
   C. was half insane and half god

2. Steinbeck uses which of the following   _____
   images in his description of the Indian
   trackers to suggest that they were
   dehumanized?
   A. excited dogs   B. crying coyotes
   C. scavenger birds

3. Kino beats Juana for stealing the pearl   _____
   because
   A. she has disobeyed him
   B. her actions have threatened his dream
   C. she has overstepped her place as a
      woman

4. From his experiences in the world, Kino   _____
   learns that the

A. established system is the best way of
   doing things
B. potential for evil lies within everyone
C. priest was right all along

5. Which of the following images does _____
   Steinbeck use to describe Kino and Juana
   when they return to the village at the end?
   A. scorpions   B. scuttling crabs
   C. towers of darkness

6. The priest's visit to Kino's hut is unusual _____
   because
   A. the priest rarely visited the Indians
   B. Kino was not Roman Catholic
   C. it was Sunday

7. Which of the following is central to the _____
   theme of appearance vs. reality?
   A. the mirages on the Gulf
   B. the image of the mountains
   C. the deceit of the pearl buyers

8. Whenever Kino deals with the Spanish, he _____
   feels
   A. disgust and superiority
   B. pity and contempt
   C. fear and anger

9. Juan Tomás hesitates to help Kino because _____
   he
   A. thinks Kino is wrong to challenge the
      system
   B. is afraid the trouble caused by the
      pearl will spread to him
   C. believes helping is not part of Indian
      customs

10. The extensive use of animal imagery in _____
    Chapter VI suggests that Kino
    A. has been dehumanized by the ordeal
       of the pearl
    B. is now outside of the natural world
    C. is worth less than an animal

11. Choose one biological comparison from *The Pearl* and explain its use.

12. Some readers see *The Pearl* as an allegory on greed. Support or refute this interpretation, citing examples from the novel.

13. How does the point of view (narrative) of *The Pearl* work to make the story seem like a retold tale?

ANSWERS

Test 1
1. A   2. C   3. C   4. B   5. A   6. B
7. C   8. C   9. A   10. B

11. The ruling class, descended from the Spanish, controlled the Indians by keeping them poor and ignorant. If Coyotito were sent to school to learn "what is in the books," he could challenge the authority of the system. He could also educate the other Indians and make them aware of ways they might fight their oppressors.

One scene that might be useful to review is the doctor's visit to Kino's hut in Chapter III. There, you see firsthand how the doctor manipulates Kino through the Indian's ignorance. Kino wants to throw the doctor out, but he can't because he doesn't know if the doctor is lying about the effects of the scorpion sting. The doctor would not have been able to carry off the capsule scene with an educated person. It is this kind of control over the Indians that educating Coyotito would change, and it is too threatening for the Spanish upper class to allow.

Another scene you might want to review is the scene at the pearl buyers. Kino's people have been dealing with pearls for centuries and certainly know the look of a valuable pearl. Yet they allow the pearl buyers' tricks to make them doubt their own judgment. If Coyotito were educated, he would be in a position to fight such financial exploitation.

12. Juan Tomás is the voice of the Indians who have survived oppression, the voice of experience. He doesn't try to stop Kino from making the dream of the pearl come true, but he does try to warn Kino that he has overestimated the powers of friendship and underestimated the dangers against him.

One place to look for details is the trip to the pearl buyers in Chapter IV. On the way, Juan Tomás reviews the situation and warns Kino that he might be cheated. He also tries to put the event in the context of tradition. It is here that Juan Tomás reminds Kino of the priest's sermon about other men who have sought to bypass the pearl buyers. Later on, when Kino says he will go to the capital, Juan Tomás warns him that he will be leaving family and friends. Here you see the concept of *mi tierra*, the ancient attachment to the place of birth, spoken by Juan Tomás. He is the spokesman for traditional Indian ways.

13. The pearl functions as a symbol on many levels. In your answer, you may want to consider the pearl as a symbol of human greed, dreams of the future, and the human soul. The idea of human greed is first developed at the beginning of Chapter III with the description of the pearl's effect on the people of the town. In discussing dreams of the future, include the list of Kino's dreams or visions, as related in Chapter III. For Kino the pearl is the key to attaining these dreams. In terms of the human soul, before Kino leaves for the mountains, he tells Juan Tomás, "This pearl has become my soul." This may mean that the pearl and its visions have taken over Kino's true soul, driving him to go against hopeless forces and to sacrifice his own family. It may also mean that Kino's only hope for dignity (his own and his people's) lies in the pearl, and without it he is less than a man.

Whatever aspect of the pearl's meaning you discuss, you should account for the significance of Kino's throwing it back in the water at the end. Also, be sure to include in your answer the contrast between the pearl's great value, beauty, and promise and its ultimate role as a catalyst of envy, greed, and destruction.

Test 2

1. C   **2.** A   **3.** B   **4.** B   **5.** C   **6.** A
7. A   **8.** C   **9.** B   **10.** A

11. There are two main biological comparisons in *The Pearl*. One compares the effect of the pearl to the scorpion's poison at the beginning of Chapter III. This comparison suggests that greed and evil are possible within each person and can come to the surface under certain circumstances. The pearl is a catalyst that brings out such characteristics in people. Steinbeck might even be suggesting that the tendency to greed and evil is inborn, a part of human nature.

The other biological comparison equates the town with a "colonial animal." This metaphor reinforces Steinbeck's claim that humans, as well as other species, are interconnected. Nothing happens to one person (a part of the village) alone. For example, Kino alone finds the pearl, but the pearl affects everyone in the village. The village itself behaves like a single organism whose single parts (each inhabitant) react to a stimulus and together contribute to the reaction of the whole (the village).

12. The greed that you witness throughout the novel, along with Kino's final gesture of renunciation, certainly suggest that the novel can be read as a warning about the burden of money and possessions. The valuable pearl brings Kino and his family to destruction. There are, however, points of conflicting evidence to suggest the beneficial aspects of material wealth. For example, Steinbeck suggests that greed is part of human nature and that it has both good and bad aspects. Greed makes a man look beyond himself to larger possibilities, as well as making him greedily covet the things of others. On the positive side, it is a good sign that human beings are always eager for improvements in their lives. This helps to assure the progress of humanity.

As a second example, Kino is humiliated and powerless in the face of the people of Spanish descent. If Steinbeck were trying to make antimaterialism his major theme, he probably would not have made Kino's fear and rage seem so justified a response to oppression.

13. Technically, the story of Kino is told by a third-person, omniscient narrator. This narrator speaks from a distance, especially in the introduction and at the end, to give the feeling of an old, retold tale. In other words, rather than hearing a firsthand story that the narrator has personally experienced, you are hearing a story told to the narrator. As the novel progresses, the point of view sometimes becomes more immediate in order to take the reader into the action (the way a movie camera does when it zooms in close). It seems as if the narrator is relating the events as they are happening. In Chapter VI, for example, you seem to be directly involved in the flight of Kino and Juana. Throughout *The Pearl*, the narrator moves back and forth between "close-up" action and distant storytelling.

Term Paper Ideas and other Topics for Writing

The Pearl and other works by Steinbeck

1. Compare and contrast the use of repeated statements about a dream in *The Pearl* and *Of Mice and Men*.

2. Discuss the role of economic and social oppression in *The Pearl* and *The Grapes of Wrath*.

3. Compare Kino's isolation to that of two other Steinbeck characters (for example, Lennie and George in *Of Mice and Men*).

Characterization

1. Do you consider the characters in *The Pearl* to be flat and stylized, or realistic?

2. Explain the conflict among the old Indian ways, nature, and "civilized" society as it exists within Kino.

3. Compare the relationship between Kino and Juana at the beginning and at the end of *The Pearl*.

Themes

1. Explain the theme of class struggle in *The Pearl*.

2. Discuss the development of social consciousness in *The Pearl*.

3. Develop one theme that might come from a feminist reading of *The Pearl*.

4. How is the theme of appearance vs. reality developed in the novel?

5. Describe the role of religion, in general, and the Catholic Church, in particular.

6. Discuss *The Pearl* as an anticapitalist novel.

Form and Structure

1. Discuss how the parable form is used in *The Pearl*.

2. Discuss the use of Steinbeck's preface as a technique in the novel. What is its purpose and effect?

3. Describe the biblical motifs in *The Pearl* and explain their effects.

4. Describe the biological metaphor of the "colonial animal" in *The Pearl* and explain its purpose.

Further Reading
CRITICAL WORKS

Davis, Murray, ed. *Steinbeck: A Collection of Critical Essays*. Englewood Cliffs, N.J.: Prentice-Hall, 1972. Critical essays on Steinbeck.

Fontenrose, Joseph. *John Steinbeck: An Introduction and Interpretation*. New York: Barnes & Noble, 1963. Forms and myth in Steinbeck's fiction.

French, Warren. *John Steinbeck*. Boston: Twayne, 1975. An interpretation of Steinbeck's works.

Jain, Sunita. *Steinbeck's Concept of Man: A Critical Study of His Novels*. Atlantic Highlands, N.J.: Humanities, 1980.

Lisca, Peter. *The Wide World of John Steinbeck*. New Brunswick: Rutgers University Press, 1958. A good overview of Steinbeck's development as an author.

McCarthy, John. *John Steinbeck*. New York: Frederick Ungar, 1980. A chronological description of Steinbeck's development as an author.

O'Connor, Richard. *John Steinbeck*. New York: McGraw-Hill, 1970. An excellent biography.

Pierre, Brian. *John Steinbeck: The California Years*. San Francisco: Chronicle Books, 1984.

AUTHOR'S OTHER MAJOR WORKS

Fiction
Cup of Gold, 1929
The Pastures of Heaven, 1932
Tortilla Flat, 1935
In Dubious Battle, 1936

The Red Pony, 1937
Of Mice and Men, 1937
The Grapes of Wrath, 1939
The Moon Is Down, 1942
Cannery Row, 1945
The Wayward Bus, 1947
Burning Bright, 1950
East of Eden, 1952
Sweet Thursday, 1954
The Short Reign Of Pippin IV, 1957
The Winter of Our Discontent, 1961

Non-Fiction

To A God Unknown, 1933
The Sea of Cortez, 1941
A Russian Journal, 1948
Travels With Charley in Search of America, 1962
America and Americans, 1966

Glossary

Algae: Water plants without true roots or stems, such as seaweed.

Bougainvillaea: Tropical shrub with inconspicuous flowers surrounded by large purple or red leaves.

Bulwark: A wall-like structure, like a breakwater, raised for defense.

Cacti: Plural of *cactus*, a thorny desert plant.

Catalyst: Something (or someone) that hastens or brings about a change or a result.

Confession: In the Catholic Church the admission of sins to a priest in order to gain forgiveness.

Eggshell china: Very delicate porcelain that is so thin it is translucent.

Escarpment: Steep slope formed by erosion or a break in the earth.

Estuary: Wide mouth of a river where the sea tide meets the river current.

Incandescence: Emission by a hot body of radiation that makes it visible.

Indigene: Native plant or animal.

Legerdemain: Deceptive performance that depends on manual dexterity; trickery or deceit.

Mangroves: Tropical trees and shrubs that tend to grow together in thick masses in swampy areas.

Monolithic: Made from a single piece of stone; suggesting an unyielding quality.

Pearl of the World: Ideal pearl; largest and most beautiful pearl in the world.

Poultice: Moist mass of cloth or vegetable matter (like herbs) applied to a sore or inflammation for medicinal purposes.

Precipitate: To separate the solid part out from a solution or the substance separated out.

Pulque: Fermented drink made from agave plants, popular in Mexico.

Seed pearls: Very small pearls that resemble grain or seeds in size and form.

Station (of the Virgin): Shrine dedicated to the Virgin Mary, to which religious pilgrimages are made.

Suppliant: One who asks earnestly or begs.

Winchester carbine: Short-barreled, lever-action rifle usually used for deer and big game, famous for its power and accuracy.

The Critics

The Source of *The Pearl*

Steinbeck nurtured the fable he heard in Mexico four years before he consciously began to develop it. The moral—that the finder of the pearl would be "free" only when he was rid of it—probably was the original inspiration because it accorded with Steinbeck's earlier beliefs that money and possessions are an intolerable burden, though he himself saw no conflict in carrying that burden. As he imagined the characters involved, they grew and changed shape; they became part of Steinbeck's story as distinct from the legend. In changing, of course, they also shaped the story into something unlike the tale as Steinbeck first heard it.

—*Richard O'Connor*, John Steinbeck, 1970

Steinbeck's Style

However meaningful the parable of the pearl may be in the abstract, Steinbeck's success in fleshing out this parable to the dimensions of a credible, forceful human adventure ultimately rests on his prose style, which is flexible to the extent that here as in most of his other novels it becomes technique as well as medium. It is capable not only of creating an aura of symbolic suggestion, but also of rendering details in terms of a camera.

—*Peter Lisca*, The Wide World of John Steinbeck, 1958

The Pearl as Sentimental

Steinbeck is trying in *The Pearl* to create a drama of the growth of conscious responsibility, but Kino's act of throwing away the pearl doesn't settle things for him as it did for the legendary fisherboy. The source offered a perfect tale of a man who consciously weighed the odds and chose hard work and poverty over being pestered all the time—a story that would have made a wonderfully tough-minded companion piece to *Cannery Row*.

Steinbeck, however, decided to give the legend some sentimental twists without realizing all the revisions that his first changes would necessitate. Perhaps such a basically fantastic, sentimental story does not warrant such strong condemnation; but *The Pearl* has been widely used as an introduction to fiction, and it provides the kind of introduction that is a disservice to its author—who wrote much better, controlled works—and to fiction itself by failing to suggest the tough-minded complexity of the greatest examples of the art.

—*Warren French*, John Steinbeck, 1975

The Pearl as an Allegory

Kino is identified symbolically with low animal orders: he must rise early and he must root in the earth for sustenance; but the simple, pastoral life has the beauty of the stars, the dawn, and the singing, happy birds. Yet provided also is a realistic description of village life on the fringe of La Paz. Finally, we should observe that the allegory too has begun. The first sentence—"Kino has awakened in the near dark"—is a statement of multiple allegorical significance. Kino is what modern sociologists are fond of calling a primitive. As such, he comes from a society that is in its infancy; or, to paraphrase Steinbeck, it is in the dark or near-dark intellectually, politically, theologically, and sociologically. But the third sentence tells us that the roosters have been crowing for some time, and we are to understand that Kino has heard the cock of progress crow. He will begin to question the institutions that have kept him primitive: medicine, the church, the pearl industry, the government. The allegory operates then locally, dealing with at first one person, Kino, and then with his people, the Mexican peasants of Lower California. But the allegory works also universally, and Kino is Everyman. The darkness in which he

awakes is one of the spirit. The cock crow is one of
warning that the spirit must awake to its own dangers.

—Harry Morris, "The Pearl: Realism
and Allegory" from Steinbeck:
A Collection of Critical Essays,
1972

NOTES

NOTES

NOTES

NOTES

NOTES

NOTES

NOTES

NOTES

NOTES

NOTES